Someone is stealing shopping bags!

Cam and Eric moved aside as a man walked past. He was carrying a big pile of school supplies. And he was reading from a list. "Crayons," he read, "not a big box, but not a small box. Tape, paste, and colored pipe cleaners."

The man looked on the floor near the notebook tower. He walked around the tower and then stopped. "Someone took my shopping bag," he said.

Cam looked at the man and said, "*Click*."

"Help! Help!" the man called. "Someone stole my shopping bag."

The man dropped what he was carrying and said, "Now don't anybody move until I get back that shopping bag."

CASE #11

The Mystery of the
Stolen Corn Popper

David A. Adler
Illustrated by Susanna Natti

SCHOLASTIC INC.

ISBN 978-0-439-13750-8

Text copyright © 1986 by David A. Adler.
Illustrations copyright © 1986 by Susanna Natti.
Logo illustration copyright © 2010 by Penguin Young Readers Group.
All rights reserved. Published by Scholastic Inc., 557 Broadway, New York, NY 10012,
by arrangement with Puffin Books, a division of Penguin Young Readers Group,
a member of Penguin Group (USA) Inc. SCHOLASTIC and associated logos
are trademarks and/or registered trademarks of Scholastic Inc.

15 14 13 12 11 10 9   13 14 15 16 17 18/0

Printed in the U.S.A.   40

First Scholastic printing, September 1999

To Lydia Eeva and
Katherine Eliina

Chapter One

"Don't push. Don't rush. There's plenty for everyone," a guard at the front of Binky's Department Store called out.

A crowd of shoppers was trying to get into Binky's. And shoppers carrying large, full, green Binky's shopping bags were trying to get out. Cam Jansen and her friend Eric Shelton were a part of the crowd going in.

"Maybe we should come back tomorrow," Eric said.

"We can't come back," Cam told him. "We need notebooks and other things for school."

BINKY'S BACK-TO-SCHOOL SALE was written in large letters on a sign in the store window. SMART STUDENTS AND THEIR PARENTS BUY AT BINKY'S. Below it was a long list of things on sale.

It was late afternoon. Cam and Eric had just finished their first day of school. They were in the same fifth-grade class.

They squeezed through the front door. They walked down a wide aisle in the Household Helpers department. People were crowded around tables covered with aprons, pot holders, light bulbs, and can openers.

"Can you tell us where to find school supplies?" Eric asked a guard. The guard was wearing a bright green uniform.

"Walk straight down this aisle until you come to a big gumdrop display. They're

on sale, you know. Make a left turn after the gumdrops. Walk past chewing gum and taffy, and you'll see a tower of notebooks. That's School Supplies."

Cam and Eric began to walk away.

"Oh, and don't take a notebook from the bottom of the tower," the guard said. "If you can't reach the top, ask someone for help."

Cam and Eric walked toward a table piled high with bags of gumdrops. People were crowded around the table. As Cam and Eric walked past the table, they heard a woman counting.

"Eleven, twelve, thirteen . . ."

"I wonder what she's counting," Eric whispered to Cam.

"I'm counting red gumdrops," the woman said. "They're my favorites. Some packages have more than others."

Cam and Eric turned left. They walked through the candy department, past the chewing gum and taffy.

"There's the notebook tower. It's not so high," Cam said.

"But look at that long line of people

4

waiting to pay for school supplies," Eric said.

Eric reached into his shirt pocket. It was empty. He reached into both pockets of his pants. "Did you bring the list?" he asked Cam. "I left mine at home."

"It's right up here," Cam said, and she pointed to her head.

Cam closed her eyes and said, *"Click."* Cam always says *"Click"* when she wants to remember something. "It's the sound a camera makes," she explains to people who wonder why she says it so often. "And my mind is a mental camera."

"We each need two notebooks," Cam said, with her eyes still closed, "a memo pad, four pencils, a large eraser, two blue pens, a ruler, index cards, and a large box of colored paper clips."

Adults say that Cam has a photographic memory. They mean that Cam remembers just about everything she sees. It's as if she has photographs stored in her brain.

Cam's real name is Jennifer Jansen. When she was very young, people called her "Red" because she has red hair. But when they found out about her amazing memory, they began calling her "The Camera." Soon "The Camera" was shortened to "Cam."

Cam opened her eyes. She and Eric took two notebooks from the top of the tower. Then they looked for memo pads.

"Excuse me," someone said. "Sorry."

Cam and Eric moved aside as a man walked past. He was carrying a big pile of school supplies. And he was reading from a list. "Crayons," he read, "not a big box, but not a small box. Tape, paste, and colored pipe cleaners."

The man looked on the floor near the notebook tower. He walked around the tower and then stopped. "Someone took my shopping bag," he said.

Cam looked at the man and said, *"Click."*

"Help! Help!" the man called. "Some-one stole my shopping bag."

The man dropped what he was carrying and said, "Now don't anybody move until I get back that shopping bag."

Chapter Two

People turned to look at the man. Two guards wearing bright green uniforms came running through the crowd.

Cam wanted to remember everyone who was nearby when the man's shopping bag was taken. She looked toward the candy department, closed her eyes, and said, *"Click."* Then Cam turned around, closed her eyes, and said *"Click"* again.

"What happened? What was taken?" one of the guards asked the man.

"Everything. Just everything. I've been

shopping for two hours. I bought two pairs of socks, blue and brown. A sweater, a flowerpot, and a present for the Morgans' fiftieth anniversary. I bought them a Binky's corn popper. Do you think that's a good present?"

"I don't know," one of the guards answered. The other guard was writing on a notepad.

"The Morgans like old movies. Whenever a good one is on TV, they stay up to watch it," the man said. "I thought they might want to eat popcorn while they watch. The corn popper was right on top. It was wrapped in gold paper with a big green bow."

The guard stopped writing. He took a walkie-talkie off his belt and spoke into it. "Attention, all exit guards. Attention. Stop anyone carrying a box wrapped in gold with a green bow."

"Now you'll have to come with us and

fill out a report," the guard told the man.

"I'm not shopping for those things all over again," the man said as he followed the guards. "Do you know how long the lines are? And I still need school supplies."

Eric whispered to Cam, "I think he lost that shopping bag."

"No," Cam said. "With all the noise he made, someone would have found it."

Cam watched as the man followed the guards. Then she looked for index cards. Eric was already looking for pens, pencils, and erasers.

Eric was reaching for a pack of pencils when Cam tapped him on his shoulder. She pointed to a woman in the candy department and whispered, "She's been looking over here for a long time."

"So?"

"I remember her. She was here when the man's shopping bag was stolen."

Eric took a pack of pencils from the display. Then he found the pens and erasers.

"Put those things down," Cam told him. "That woman is holding a shopping bag, and I'll bet she has a corn popper in there."

Eric put down the school supplies. He followed Cam past the notebook tower.

They stopped at a display of candy canes and lollipops.

"She was right here," Cam said.

Eric pointed. "There she is."

The woman was looking at boxes of iced cookies and cakes. Cam and Eric watched her. Then the woman walked through the Care for Your Hair department, and Cam and Eric followed her.

Cam and Eric were careful not to get too close to the woman. There were always a few shoppers between them and her.

They followed the woman to the baby department. The woman looked at bottles, baby spoons, and diaper sets. Then she stopped in front of a rack of very small dresses. She put the shopping bag down and took one of the dresses off the rack. She looked at the dress and put it back. Then the woman walked down the aisle to look at other baby clothes.

"Let's go," Cam whispered. "She left the shopping bag. Now's our chance to look inside."

Chapter Three

Cam and Eric walked toward the shopping bag.

"Can I help you?" someone asked.

Cam and Eric looked up. A woman wearing a bright green dress with a large white button was standing in front of them. HELLO. MY NAME IS ANN. I'M A BINKY'S HELPER was printed on the button.

"We don't need any help," Cam told Ann.

Cam and Eric started to walk toward the shopping bag again.

"We have some charming rattles," Ann said. "They make wonderful gifts. And we have some very pretty diaper sets."

"No, thank you. We don't need help," Cam said.

"Maybe you'd like to buy the baby a stuffed animal. We have teddy bears, giraffes, monkeys, turtles, parrots, cats, and elephants."

"I'll look at the stuffed animals," Eric told Ann.

"And I'll look at the baby dresses," Cam said.

Eric walked with Ann to the stuffed-animal display. She showed him a large pink elephant wearing blue overalls, and a green monkey in a bathing suit.

Cam took a dress off the rack and pretended to look at it. She was really looking into the shopping bag. There were two scarves in the bag and a pair of gloves. There was nothing wrapped in gold paper.

"Hey!" someone called out. "Who stole my things?"

Cam ran to Eric. "Did you hear that?" she asked. "It came from the toy department."

Cam ran off. Eric smiled at Ann and said, "No, I don't think I'll buy a stuffed animal." Then he followed Cam.

The toy department was crowded with large displays of toys on sale. A great many people were there. Some were carrying shopping bags. Cam looked at them all and said, *"Click."*

A teenage girl, dressed in purple, was near the electric train display. A long toy train was riding in a circle through the display. And each time, before the train went through the tunnel, the whistle sounded.

The girl dressed in purple was walking in circles, too, and she was talking very fast.

"Someone took my shopping bag. I know someone took it," she said. "It was right here. There was a puzzle book in that bag and some records. And I paid for all of it with my own money. I did baby-sitting so I could buy those things. I want them back."

"Toot, toot," the train whistle sounded.

"I called for one of the guards," a Binky's Helper told the girl.

"You tell him that I want my things back," the girl said. "You just tell him."

A few of the people standing nearby were waiting to see what would happen. Others walked away.

Cam looked at all the people walking away and told Eric, "One of those people stole her shopping bag. I'm sure of it. I just don't know which one."

"*Toot, toot.*"

A Binky's guard rushed past Cam and Eric. She asked the girl some questions.

"I don't know who took the bag," the girl said. She was still walking in circles. "I just know it's mine. And I want it back."

Cam whispered to Eric, "I have pictures stored in my head of all the people who were nearby when the corn popper was taken. And I have pictures of the people who were here."

"So?"

"Whoever stole the girl's bag probably took the other one, too. And I think I can find out who it was. I just have to look at my pictures and see who was in both places."

"Then do it!" Eric said.

Cam closed her eyes and said, *"Click."*

"Toot, toot."

Cam opened her eyes and said, "I can't think here. It's too noisy."

Eric said, "Let's go to the snack bar. You can think there. And I'm thirsty."

Cam and Eric walked through the store. They saw long lines of people waiting to pay for things. In the clothing department, people were trying on hats and sweaters and looking in mirrors.

At the snack bar, Cam and Eric sat on stools. "I'll have a small cup of ginger ale," Eric told the waitress.

"What does your friend want?"

Cam's eyes were closed. She said, *"Click."* She said *"Click"* again.

"What's a *'Click'*?" the waitress asked. "I don't think we have that kind of soda."

"Then just bring her some ginger ale," Eric told her.

Cam's eyes were still closed when the

waitress brought the cups of soda. Eric paid for the drinks. He drank his.

Cam said *"Click"* again. Then she opened her eyes and said, "I know who it is. I know who stole those shopping bags."

Chapter Four

Cam got off her stool and walked quickly through the clothing department. She was looking for a guard. Eric ran after her.

"Who is it? What does he look like?" Eric asked her.

"It's a *her*," Cam said as she walked up to a guard in the men's shirt department.

"I know who stole the shopping bags," Cam told the guard. "It's a woman with long, curly brown hair, glasses, and a blue dress with flowers on it."

The guard was a very tall man. He looked down at Cam.

"Didn't anyone call and tell you about the stolen shopping bags?" Cam asked.

"Yes."

"Well, I know who stole them. It was a woman with long, curly brown hair, glasses, and a blue dress with flowers on it."

The man smiled.

Eric said, "I think you should call the other guards and tell them. Cam has an amazing memory. She has used it to solve mysteries just like this one."

"Guard! Guard!" someone called. "Come over here, please."

The guard ran to the men's shirt display. Cam and Eric followed him. A Binky's Helper was holding a small boy. The boy was crying.

"He's lost," the Binky's Helper said.

The guard smiled at the child and

24

asked, "Is your mother or father here?"

"Mama," the boy said.

"Where is she? What is she buying?"

"Dirt."

"Dirt!" the Binky's Helper said. "Why would anyone buy dirt?"

"He must mean potting soil," the guard said. "We sell it in our Household Helpers department. I'll take him there."

The guard took the small boy in his

arms. The boy looked up at the guard and cried.

"Let's go," the guard said. He took big, quick steps. Shoppers moved aside. The boy continued to cry as he was carried to the Household Helpers department.

Cam and Eric followed them. "Don't you want to know who stole the shopping bags?" Cam asked.

The guard didn't answer.

Eric said, "He can't hear you. That boy is crying too loud."

The guard carried the boy to a table covered with houseplants. Next to the plants were watering cans, clay pots, and potting soil.

The boy stopped crying.

"Now can I tell you who stole the shopping bags?" Cam asked.

"Not now! I'm looking for this boy's mother."

The boy began to cry again.

"Let's go," Cam said to Eric. "We'll find another guard."

As Cam and Eric looked for another guard, the soft music that was playing throughout the store stopped. "Attention, shoppers. Attention, shoppers," someone announced. "For the next hour, in our Binky's Happy Feet department, all shoes are on sale at half the regular price. That's right, shoppers. All shoes are on sale."

Two men and a woman ran down the Household Helpers aisle. Cam and Eric stepped aside to let them pass. Another woman came running toward Cam and Eric. Her coat flew open as she ran. She had one hand on her head to keep her hat from flying off. With her other hand she carried a shopping bag. The woman ran right past Cam and Eric. Then she stopped.

"Which way are the shoes?" she asked.

Eric pointed down the aisle. "Everyone is going that way," he said.

The woman thanked Eric and ran off.

Cam and Eric walked slowly along the side of the aisle as shoppers ran past them.

Cam and Eric walked toward an exit. "There's a guard," Cam said. "And look! Look! He's caught her. He's caught the woman in the blue dress."

Chapter Five

The guard was talking to a woman in a blue dress. But as Cam and Eric walked closer, they saw that the woman was wearing a brown hat. She didn't have brown hair. And there were no flowers on her dress.

"We sell dried fruit in our candy department," the guard was telling the woman. "Just walk down this aisle and you'll come right to it."

The woman said, "Thank you," and walked away.

"I know who stole the shopping bags," Cam told the guard. "It's a woman with long, curly brown hair, glasses, and a blue dress with flowers on it."

The guard smiled at Cam. "What makes you think you know who stole those shopping bags?" he asked.

Eric said, "Cam has an amazing memory. She says *'Click'* and remembers just about everything she sees. Cam remembers seeing that woman leaving School Supplies with a shopping bag just after the corn popper was taken. And she was leaving Toys when the records and puzzle book were stolen."

The guard asked, "How can you be so sure it was the same woman?"

"I told you. She has an amazing memory," Eric said. "Go on, Cam. Show him."

Cam looked at the guard. Then she closed her eyes and said *"Click."*

"You're wearing a green uniform," Cam

said with her eyes closed. Your badge says 'Binky's Security Guard, Number 397.' And you had ketchup for lunch."

"That's right. I did. You *do* have an amazing memory."

Cam opened her eyes. "You should move that badge to cover the ketchup."

The guard laughed. "I can't," he said. "It's covering a mustard stain from yesterday's lunch."

The guard took a memo pad from his pocket and said, "Now tell me about that woman."

Cam described the woman. The guard wrote down the description. Then he said, "After she stole that first shopping bag, we were looking for her. We didn't know what she looked like, but we knew she had a gift wrapped in gold paper with a green bow. But she never left the store. Now she's carrying two stolen shopping bags. We'll find her."

As Cam and Eric walked away they heard the guard talk into his walkie-talkie. He gave Cam's description of the thief to the other store guards.

"They'll catch her now," Eric said. "Let's hurry and get the notebooks, pencils, and things. I have to be home in time for supper."

As they walked through the Household Helpers department, Cam pointed to someone in the Happy Feet department and said, "Look at that woman. She's wearing a blue dress."

Cam and Eric walked closer. There were flowers on the woman's dress, and she had brown hair. Cam and Eric waited for her to turn around. When she did, Cam looked right at the woman, blinked her eyes, and said, *"Click."*

"She's wearing glasses," Eric said.

Cam closed her eyes and said *"Click"* again.

"That's her," Cam said as she opened her eyes. "Let's go!"

Eric walked closely behind Cam. He whispered, "Why don't we tell a guard?"

"First let's make sure she's the thief. Let's see if she has the two stolen shopping bags."

The woman walked slowly through the Happy Feet department. She looked down a lot, as if she were looking for something.

But she wasn't carrying any shopping bags.

The woman left Happy Feet and walked into Household Helpers. She walked right past Cam and Eric.

"I don't understand it," Cam whispered. "She was there whenever a shopping bag was stolen. I was sure she was the thief."

"Well, she didn't have the shopping bags, so she's not," Eric said. "And we should tell the guards not to stop her."

Cam and Eric walked into the Household Helpers department again. They saw the very tall guard and walked toward him. They planned to tell him that the woman in the blue dress was not the thief. The small boy was still in the guard's arms. The guard hadn't found the boy's mother.

Eric stopped. He looked at the tall guard. Eric rubbed his chin and said, "I just remembered something. And I think I know where that boy's mother is."

Cam and Eric walked up to the guard. Eric pointed to the front of his own shirt and asked the boy, "What is this?"

The guard and the boy looked down at Eric.

Eric pointed to his shirt again and asked, "What is this?"

"Dirt," the boy said.

"Dirt? You mean shirt!" the guard said. "Your mother isn't buying dirt. She's buying a shirt."

The guard took big, quick steps as he walked to the clothing department. Cam and Eric followed him.

"How did you know 'dirt' meant 'shirt'?" Cam asked Eric as they walked.

"That boy reminds me of my sisters. When Donna and Diane were little, it was hard to know what they were saying. 'Dees' was 'keys,' and 'gogul' was 'bottle.'"

The guard walked past the men's shirts, neckties, and pants displays. Then, as he was walking past a table covered with sweaters, the boy called out, "Mama."

"Andy," a woman answered. She ran toward him. "Where have you been? I've been looking everywhere for you."

"Mama."

"Thank you so much," the woman said to the guard as she took the boy in her arms.

"Mama."

"Don't thank me," the guard told her. "This boy told me where to find you."

"Thank you," the woman said to Eric.

The soft music that was playing throughout the store stopped again. "Attention, shoppers. Attention, shoppers," someone announced. "For the next thirty minutes, in our Binky's Looking Good clothing department, all men's shirts are on sale at half our regular price. That's right, shoppers. All men's shirts are on sale."

"We'd better get out of the way," Cam said.

Shoppers were already rushing to the clothing department. Then Cam and Eric heard someone call out, "Help! My shopping bag has been stolen!"

Chapter Six

"Quick!" Cam said. "That came from over there, the gift department."

Cam and Eric ran toward the gift department. And men and women were running toward Cam and Eric, to get to the men's shirts. Most of them were careful not to run into Cam or Eric. But one very fat man carrying two shopping bags wasn't careful at all. He ran straight down the aisle shouting, "Get out of my way! Get out of my way!"

Cam and Eric moved aside to let the fat

man pass. Then Cam pointed and said, "There she is again!"

Cam was pointing to the woman with long, curly brown hair, glasses, and a blue dress with flowers on it. She was leaving the gift department. She was walking quickly. And she kept turning and looking behind her as she walked.

"She *must* be the thief," Cam said to

Eric. "She's there every time a shopping bag is stolen."

"But what does she do with the shopping bags?"

"Let's follow her," Cam said. "There she is, behind that rack of men's jackets."

Cam and Eric began to cross the aisle. A woman came running toward them. Cam and Eric moved aside. The woman's coat flew open as she ran. She had one hand on her head to keep her hat from flying off. In her other hand she was holding two shopping bags. It was the same woman Cam and Eric had seen near the shoe sale.

"Which way are the shirts?" she asked.

Cam pointed to the men's shirt display. Then she looked for the woman in the blue dress. Cam ran to the jacket rack. Eric ran past the jackets to the men's coats, neckties, and sweaters. The woman was gone.

"Let's get to the exit before she does," Cam said.

Cam and Eric ran to the nearest exit. The guard standing there was a woman. Her arms were folded.

"Did she come here?" Cam asked quickly. "Did she leave?"

"Who?"

"The woman in the blue dress. She stole the shopping bags."

Eric spoke more slowly. "A woman in a blue dress has been stealing shopping bags. She just stole another one. And she was coming this way."

The guard reached into her pocket and took out her memo pad. She read from it and asked, "Does that woman have long, curly brown hair and glasses?"

"Yes."

"All the exit guards are looking for her. She hasn't left the store."

"She will," Cam said. "She's coming here

now with another stolen shopping bag."

Cam and Eric stood by the guard and waited. Shoppers walked past them as they came into the store. Others left carrying full Binky's shopping bags.

"She should have been here by now," Eric said.

Cam watched as a short woman carrying four loaded shopping bags, two in each hand, tried to get through the door. Then Cam said, "Maybe she has a secret way to get out of the store. Or maybe she puts on a disguise before she leaves."

Eric whispered, "Or maybe she's a partner with a guard at one of the exits and the guard lets her go past."

The music stopped again. "Attention, all shoppers. For the next ten minutes only, with every five-pound box of taffy you buy, you get a free two-pound bag of jelly beans. That's right, shoppers, free jelly beans."

A woman carrying a full Binky's shopping bag was walking into the store. "Where is that?" she asked the guard. "Where are those free jelly beans?"

The guard told the woman how to get to the candy department. Cam watched as the woman walked off. Cam rubbed her chin and thought for a moment. Then she told Eric, "Come with me. I think I know where to find the shopping-bag thief."

Chapter Seven

"**W**here are we going?" Eric asked.

"That woman carrying the shopping bag *into* the store made me think," Cam said as they walked.

"What's there to think about?" Eric asked. "That woman probably forgot to buy something, so she came back. That's why she was walking into the store carrying a shopping bag."

"Maybe," Cam said, "and maybe not."

Eric followed Cam to the other end of the store. They walked through the cur-

tain, sheet, and towel department to Gift
Wrap and Returns.

Cam looked at the long lines of people
waiting to return something they had
bought. Then she found her. The woman
in the blue dress was in the middle of the
last line.

"There she is," Cam whispered.

"Now I understand why she didn't have the corn popper when we saw her," Eric whispered. "As soon as she steals a shopping bag, she returns whatever is in it and keeps the money."

Cam said, "And that's why none of the exit guards saw her. She never left the store."

Then Cam told Eric, "I'll wait here. You get one of the guards."

Eric took a few steps away. Then he came back. "I think I'll get Guard Number 397, the one with the ketchup stain. I know he'll come."

Eric walked off. Cam stood at the end of one of the other lines and watched the woman.

There were two shoppers in line ahead of the woman in the blue dress. Cam watched as a woman behind the Returns counter gave the money to the first shopper in line. The man counted the money and walked away. Everyone in the last line moved a step closer to the Returns counter. Now there was only one shopper ahead of the woman in the blue dress.

An old man lifted a large suitcase onto the Returns counter. He spoke to the woman behind the counter and then showed her the zipper on the suitcase. The woman took the suitcase and returned the money he had paid. The old man smiled and walked away. Now the woman in the blue dress stepped up to the counter.

The woman in the blue dress took a box and a receipt out of the shopping bag and put them on the counter. Then she took two more boxes from the bag and put them on the counter, too.

Cam looked into the curtain, sheet, and towel department to see if Eric was coming with the guard. He wasn't.

The woman behind the Returns counter

gave the woman in the blue dress some money. The woman in the blue dress smiled and walked quickly away. She walked past Cam.

"Excuse me," Cam said as she ran in front of the woman, "do you know where I can find the taffy?"

"I'm sorry, I don't," the woman said.

"If you buy taffy, you get free jelly beans. Don't you like jelly beans?" Cam asked.

"I don't like jelly beans. I don't like taffy. And I'm in a hurry," the woman said. "Now, will you please get out of my way?"

The woman gently pushed Cam aside and walked off. Cam ran ahead of her and asked, "Have you ever tasted a red jelly bean? They're really good."

"I told you, I'm in a hurry. I have no time for jelly beans."

"What's your hurry?" someone asked. It was Guard Number 397. Eric was with him.

"I have shopping to do."

"You mean you have stealing to do. We know about the shopping bags."

The woman started to run. But two other guards were walking up the aisle. They caught her.

A woman with red hair and a bright green dress walked quickly up to the guards. "Come with me," she said.

The guards and the shopping-bag thief followed the woman with the red hair. She turned to see that they were all behind her. Then she pointed to Cam and Eric and said, "You, too."

Chapter Eight

Cam and Eric followed the woman into a large office. The curtains, the walls, the carpet, and the chairs in the office were all green.

"I'm Betty Binky," the woman in green told the shopping-bag thief. "This is my store, and people like you are bad for business. First, you are going to return all the money you got for the things you stole."

The thief took some bills and coins

from her purse and gave them to Betty Binky.

"And now," Betty Binky said, "you'll be taken to our security office."

The guards took the thief out of the office. When they were gone, Betty Binky smiled at Cam and Eric.

"You're the two children who helped us catch that woman, aren't you?"

"Yes," Cam said. "But she almost got away. We were looking for someone carrying the stolen shopping bags. We thought she would try to leave the store with them. And when we saw her without the stolen bags, we thought we made a mistake."

"What will happen to that woman?" Eric asked.

"We'll call the police. She may go to jail."

Betty Binky smiled again and asked, "Now what did you come here to buy?"

Cam closed her eyes and said, *"Click."*

"She has an amazing memory," Eric whispered to Betty Binky. "Cam always says *'Click'* when she wants to remember something."

"I know," Betty Binky whispered to Eric. "Mike Coats told me. He's Guard Number 397."

"We each need two notebooks," Cam said with her eyes still closed, "a memo pad, four pencils, a large eraser, two blue pens, a ruler, index cards, and a large box of colored paper clips."

Betty Binky made a list of all those items. Then she pressed a button on her desk. The office door opened, and two Binky's Helpers, wearing green dresses, came in. Betty Binky gave them the list and said, "Please, get all these things, and two Binky's surprise packages."

After the two women had left, Betty Binky said to Cam and Eric, "Your teacher must be Ms. Benson. She's the only one who asks for colored paper clips. She worked here when she was in college. She's very nice."

Cam looked around the office and then said, "You really like green, don't you?"

"I *love* green," Betty Binky said. "Grass is green. Leaves are green. And my eyes are green."

Just then, the office doors opened. The Binky's Helpers carried in two shopping bags with the school supplies and the surprise packages. Eric opened one of the surprise packages.

"Candy," Eric said as he reached into the package, "gumdrops, jelly beans, lollipops, and taffy."

"And it's all green," Cam said.

"Green is the best color for dresses, carpets, and chairs," Betty Binky said. "And it's the best flavor for candy."

Cam and Eric each bit into a gumdrop. "This is good," Cam said.

"Of course it's good," Betty Binky said, and laughed. "It's green."

Cam and Eric laughed, too. Then they shared their green candy with Betty Binky and the two Binky's Helpers.